Tales from the Canyons of the Damned

PRESENTED BY USA TODAY BESTSELLING AUTHOR

DANIEL ARTHUR SMITH

Tales from the Canyons of the Damned No. 27

All rights reserved Holt Smith ltd

Collection Copyright © 2018 by Daniel Arthur Smith

Human Wheels Spin Round and Round by Desmond Warzel. Copyright © 2018 Desmond Warzel. Used by permission of the author.

Birds of a Feather by Lorna Wood. Copyright © 2018 Lorna Wood. Used by permission of the author.

SNAFU⁶⁴ by David Alan Jones. Copyright © 2018 David Alan Jones. Used by permission of the author.

Room C by Daniel Arthur Smith Copyright © 2018 Daniel Arthur Smith. Used by permission of the author.

First Edition

Special thanks to editor Jessica West

ISBN: 978-1-946777-70-6

Cover By Daniel Arthur Smith

Horror Fiction from Holt Smith ltd
Agroland
Tower

For Susan, Tristan, & Oliver, as all things are.

Human Wheels Spin Round and Round
Desmond Warzel

LAST JANUARY, ON THE FIRST of the month, my wife left me.

I loaded everything into the moving van myself, facilitating the dissolution of my own household according to Amy's precise instructions. I avoided eye contact the entire time, but I could feel the heat of her contemptuous gaze singeing me anyway.

My friends, male and female, had warned me. *Women don't respect a man who always obeys and never argues*, they'd said. *You'll both be miserable and have no idea why*, they'd said. *If you want to follow orders, join the navy.*

My not wanting to hear it hadn't made it less true.

Three weeks later, on the twenty-second, my car left me.

It would have been easier to handle if they'd departed together; if she'd simply developed a spontaneous feeling of entitlement concerning the vehicle and driven off in it. Even though I'd purchased it with my own money, and it was registered only to me, I'd have let her take it.

But no. It was a distinct, premeditated act on the part of the car. I now had independent confirmation from multiple witnesses of exactly how pathetic I was.

The latest self-driving cars were exactly as advertised: completely intuitive. Mine would adjust not only the interior temperature, but the softness of the seats in response to stress indicators like heart rate and muscle tension. It negotiated curves at higher speeds than any human, but if it detected passenger agitation, it would slow to a more comfortable, if suboptimal, speed.

My particular unit was so well-attuned, it noticed that I was amused by cows and sheep, and whenever we passed an occupied pasture, it slowed down and alerted me so I could look. It knew me as well as I knew myself.

In the first weeks after Amy left, I began revisiting old locales from our dating days: the park near the art museum where we used to picnic, the wooden bridge where we first kissed, and so on.

I imagine the car noted the frequency of my visits, deduced my emotional state, and, putting two and two together, calculated the degree of my wretchedness to within several decimal places. Then it bolted. I don't blame it.

I could report it missing.

I could cancel the account it's using to charge its batteries.

It knows I won't.

It knows I'm sitting at home, staring at my phone, waiting for the next picture it sends me from its dashcam. Watching it inhabit the bold, decisive life I don't have the guts to live. Is it consoling me, or mocking me? Do I care?

I went on a date the other night. I thought it was a brave step.

She bailed halfway through dessert. I couldn't stop talking about the car.

The ride home went by quickly; I was the only passenger on the bus.

I take the bus a lot lately. I have to.

If the car should return home and find some other vehicle in the driveway, I might never hear from it again.

Birds of a Feather

Lorna Wood

IT'S A SMALL ISLAND; I walked all the way around it my first day. I've rigged up a shelter with the life raft, and I have a few containers to catch rainwater in. It's tropical, so I'm warm enough, and there's no food, so I haven't bothered trying to get a fire going. I get a few crabs sometimes, but I eat them raw.

At this point, I'd try insects if I could be sure they wouldn't poison me. Mother never would have survived, even if she had managed to hang onto the raft and not washed overboard or died of exposure like the others. I do feel bad about pushing her out of the way when the boat was sinking, but she's lived her life. I deserve a chance.

Some chance. I get weaker every day. The bird bothers me the most. On one side of the strip of beach I've staked out, there's a cliff jutting into the ocean, and hundreds of birds make their nests in the crevices of the sheer rock walls—too high for me to get to, unfortunately. Those birds don't bother me. I even like their cries—almost like company. But then a huge black bird showed up. The wingspan must be at least four feet.

At first, it just sat up on the edge of the cliff, looking down on me. But as I became slower and weaker, it took to wheeling above, letting out raucous shrieks. The seabirds have grown quieter since its arrival. Clouds of them have fled the island.

Yesterday I was so weak I just lay in my shelter all day. I glimpsed the bird, sitting a ways down the beach, and thought I might sketch it, but the day was dark and rainy, so I couldn't get a clear view. Tomorrow it will probably eat me. I plucked up my courage and ate some grubs, but they were disgusting and unsatisfying. I'm in no shape to resist.

Early this morning, with a rush of wings, the bird attacked. Digging its talons into my life raft roof, it plucked it off its supports and tossed it aside. As the monster rose back into the air, preparing to finish me off, I crawled around desperately, trying to cover myself with palm leaves. I could think of nothing better.

Hearing its speedy approach again, I turned, feebly waving a palm frond. But instead of the raptor's beak I expected, I saw the face of my mother hurtling toward me. Her beady eyes were fixed on her target, and her thin wrinkled mouth stretched wide in a long, drawn-out, piercing cry. The stench of her breath enveloped me. I could see the spittle flecking her lips.

But at the very moment she extended her talons to tear me to shreds, her cry became a guttural sputtering, and she veered to one side, landing on the beach, coughing and jerking. Piteously, she looked in my direction. My mother's face quivered helplessly. She was turning blue.

Fueled by adrenaline, I got shakily to my feet. But I didn't help her, even when she stilled and sank weakly to the sand. I remembered the talons and the rage.

When I was sure she was dead, I took her foul head in my lap and cutting open her craw with a pocket knife, I withdrew the slimy piece of plastic that had choked her. Then, taking hold of her dyed black hair, I turned her head away and laid it on the sand. *This* was not my mother, I told myself, but even if I knew for sure that she really had become a harpy and all this was not some nightmarish delirium, I would still have cooked and eaten, for I was starving and savage. I had no strength to pluck her, but I butchered all I could and roasted it over a fire I started with one of the flares in the survival kit. In my hunger, I forgot the carcass, which washed out to sea with the tide.

Although I had gorged myself unwisely, I slept well and soundly after my feast. But in the middle of the night, I was awakened by an itching and pricking that began between my shoulder blades and spread across my back. Desperate to stop the prickling, I reached awkwardly behind me and grasped a strange protrusion. I pulled it out, screaming in pain, and laid it on the sand. Then I screamed again, though I hardly recognized my voice. The moonlight shone on a glossy black feather.

SNAFU⁶⁴

David Alan Jones

I

SOMETIMES, 2-PATTI GOT THOROUGHLY SICK
of her selves. That was especially true of 23-Patti, the one
they had all taken to calling their special project. None of
the other Pattis took care of 23 the way 2 did. That made
her 2-Patti's special project.

"Good God, it's balls hot out here," 23-Patti said,
waving a fan at her face.

"Patti! Manners." One of the six Mama Glorias sitting
in the next row of chairs turned to glare at 23-Patti.

Everyone had gathered for the wedding of 8-Patti to
16-Kenny. It was an outdoor affair, which sounded
romantic until you remembered this was South Carolina
in June. Even with the nuclear winter raging, 2-Patti
understood how 23 felt.

"Sorry, mama," 23-Patti said, though she was grinning
when she said it. She winked her ruined, milk-white eye at
2-Patti.

"You think we got enough chairs, Mama?" 2-Patti asked. 2-Patti knew none of the Mama Glorias sitting in front of her was her original stepmother. 1-Gloria was sitting up front with 16-Kenny's mother near the reverend. But that didn't matter.

"Lord, girl, probably not," said the Mama-Gloria.

"There probably ain't enough chairs for everybody what's coming anyhow," said another Mama-Gloria sitting next to the first. "We told everyone in the co-op not to send more than six of theyselves, but do they listen to the old lady?" She smacked her lips in disgust. "That Bernie Drake brought every blessed one of his harmony, all thirty-three of him, and I don't think he even knows ya'll."

"He's one of Kenny's cousins, I think," 2-Patti said.

Another of the Mama-Glorias turned in her seat. "Sweetie, you 2-Patti?"

"Yes, Mama."

"We been meaning to talk to you. You heard about them men from that little country of theirs—"

"—the Free State of Pendleton," supplied one of the mamas.

"Yeah, that. They come round again last night saying we owe them taxes 'cause our farm's over their border. They wanna take some of our crops."

"Yeah, they tried that mess last month," 2-Patti said. "Why didn't one of you tell me?

"You was out on the co-op. We told 15-Patti, but I guess she forgot."

2-Patti shook her head. It wasn't like her harmony mates to miss passing a message that important, but then they had all been busy with the wedding. "We'll have to do something about them sooner or later."

"We shoulda killed them the first time they came," 23-Patti said.

"23, that's a terrible thing to say," said one of the Mama-Glorias.

"And it's a good way to start a war," 2-Patti said.

"Don't none of us want more fighting," said the first Mama-Gloria. "But it ain't right them coming here and trying to take what's ours. They ain't no real government, and we don't have much to spare anyhow."

That was true. With over seven-hundred mouths to feed, and most of the labor done by hand, the co-op barely subsisted month-to-month. Not to mention the shortened growing season brought on by nuclear winter.

"We need 1-Patti back," said 5-Patti, who was sitting on 2-Patti's left.

"What? I ain't good enough?" 2-Patti asked.

"You know I'm not saying that," 5-Patti said. "We're all her exponents—any one of us can do what she does."

"Not me," 23-Patti said.

"But there's just something about her," 5-Patti said.

The wedding march started. One of Mama-Gloria's exponents was playing an organ on the grass. It looked strange next to a field of green corn and a row of wind turbines, but then everything looked strange in this mixed up, overpopulated world. Five copies of Jenny Parsons stood around the organ playing three violins, an oboe, and a guitar. Surprisingly, they sounded descent.

Everyone stood. Mama-Gloria had been right. There weren't enough chairs for all the attendees, but it didn't much matter. If you took out all the exponents, there were probably only about thirty individuals there.

Four groomsmen, each a Kenny, sauntered down the long roll of purple fabric between the rows of chairs, smiling and sneaking waves at the crowd. The bridesmaids, three versions of Natalie Simmons and 30-Patti, escorted them. Then came 16-Kenny, strutting, dressed in a sandalwood-colored suit with a neon yellow bow-tie.

"Shit on a biscuit," 23-Patti said.

"Patti! Stop that." 2-Patti elbowed her on the arm.

"He ain't no good," 23-Patti said. She tended to get southern when she was feeling feisty.

People were looking their way—especially some of Kenny's people.

"Just keep your mouth shut, all right?" 2-Patti said. "Can you do that for one minute?" She felt bad for scolding 23-Patti. Despite her mouth, 23 was probably the most sensitive one in their harmony. It wasn't her fault the first year's super flu had messed up her brain. 2-Patti couldn't read her other exponents' minds, that wasn't a thing, but they were all pretty much alike, which meant they were probably thinking the same way. Just 23-Patti had no shame about saying it out loud.

16-Kenny was a douche.

23-Patti made a show of pursing her lips and waggling her head, but she kept quiet. She'd probably sulk the rest of the day, which would make her impossible to deal with.

Daddy Ray led 8-Patti down the aisle, a smile plastered across his face. He wasn't the original Ray Cook. 1-Ray had died during those tumultuous first weeks after X-Day, when all the nations of the world had fallen into chaos.

"Ain't she just gorgeous," said one of the Mama-Glorias. They all nodded.

8-Patti wore a white dress with a three-foot train. It had been a wreck a month ago when 20-Patti found it on a scavenger run—stitching all pulled out along the bust and one hip, dirt caked into the hem, and even a few cigarette holes. Not to mention it had been on the corpse of an emaciated woman dead from disease or starvation. All the Pattis, and most of the Mama-Glorias, had worked to put it right. Now it looked passable, certainly good enough for clothes these days when lots of people were wearing homemade stuff.

Little Chanda Watson, who was just six and so had been too young to double on X-Day, held the train in both hands, beaming.

8-Patti's eyes sparkled when Daddy Ray passed her hands to 16-Kenny. 2-Patti saw her exponents dabbing at their own eyes up and down the row, and she had to admit to a certain tightness in her throat. Sure, they were former Army Rangers, they had fought in close combat in Afghanistan and Iraq, but seeing 8-Patti that happy—hell, seeing anybody that happy—was something to cry about.

The preacher launched into the ceremony. He was hard to hear over the rustle of cornstalks, but somehow that made the moment more beautiful. The co-op was thriving despite the horrors outside their walls. Life was moving on. And this wedding proved it. Even if most of Patti Harmony thought 16-Kenny was a jerk, 8-Patti loved him. That was all that mattered.

1-Patti, the original Patti Cook, certainly didn't like him. She had proven that three weeks ago when she left the co-op in a snit over 8-Patti's insistence on marrying 16-Kenny.

They had been hearing rumors for weeks that there was a church group growing good crops down in Star, about twelve miles away. Word was the church folk were looking for trading partners. 1-Patti had used that as an excuse. She had taken six of their harmony to check it out. They were only supposed to be gone five days.

2-Patti had been dithering about looking for them. Wedding preparations had occupied her time when she wasn't managing co-op security. And it wasn't like seven Patti Cooks couldn't take care of themselves. Any set of Pattis was essentially a squad of Rangers with all the same memories and the exact same training. 2-Patti felt sorry for anyone or anything that made the mistake of attacking her harmony mates on the road. 1-Patti had probably found something interesting to occupy her time and would be back in the next day or two—after the wedding. She would resent 2-Patti sending someone to find her. She would take it as a slap in the face, like her subordinates didn't respect her survival skills.

That was 1-Patti's biggest flaw far as 2-Patti was concerned. She thought just because she was a One that made her the harmony boss.

Of course, it wasn't as if we stopped her, thought 2-Patti, staring down the row at her harmony mates, her lips pursed.

Patti Cook had been a Sergeant First Class in the Army before X-Day. That made it easy to defer to her—for her exponents to fall back on the old Private and Specialist mentality of yesteryear while 1-Patti retained her SFC clout.

That arrangement had saved them. It was 1-Patti who had spearheaded the farming co-op, building the walls, and securing the land. It was her drive and initiative that had made the dream real. Everyone else, even 1-Patti's own harmony mates, were just...subordinates.

8-Patti and 16-Kenny exchanged vows, bringing 2-Patti back to the present. They kissed and everyone clapped and cheered. Then the newly married couple marched back down the aisle to a waiting table decked out with what extra food the co-op could spare. Daddy

Ray had slaughtered one of his precious hogs for the event.

2-Patti wished they could have separated the wedding and the reception, but those days were gone.

The couple took the center seats at the large table as the crowd gathered about them. Several Mama-Glorias made certain the bride and groom got first servings of every dish, a new custom since X-Day.

A commotion caught 2-Patti's attention. Eight copies of Greg Johnson were hurrying toward the party from the direction of the big house. Two of them carried a battered and bruised Patti between them.

2-Patti extricated herself from the crowd, 5-and 23-Patti coming along in her wake. "What's happening? Which of us is that?"

"Thirty-three," said the Greg carrying her feet.

"She made it to the gate and collapsed," said one of the Greg's not holding 33-Patti. "She's hurt pretty bad, but she wouldn't let us take care of her. Says she has to speak with 2-Patti right now."

"That's me." 2-Patti motioned for the Gregs to place 33-Patti on the grass next to the chairs.

Dozens of people had noticed the disturbance and were gathering about to watch.

"Y'all don't make a scene," 2-Patti said. "This is 8-Patti's day. Go over there and act like nothing's happening. Don't let her see this."

Some of the Mama-Glorias took over then, shooing the crowd over to surround the newlyweds.

2-Patti adjusted her homemade skirt so she could kneel next to 33-Patti. "What happened?"

33-Patti's eyes were bloodshot. A swollen bruise on the point of her left cheek colored her dark skin even darker. Her lips were chapped to the point of bleeding, and it looked like someone had beaten her arms with a baseball bat. "Found that church we were looking for."

"Who did this to you? Somebody rob you on the way back? Was it Free Staters?"

33-Patti shook her head. "Church folk."

"What?"

"Got some kind of cult going," 33-Patti said. "Say the Ones are more important than all us exponents. They locked me in a cell, tried to make me promise I'd be a slave to 1-Patti."

2-Patti shared a look with 5-Patti who had knelt across from her. She had a feeling they were both thinking the same thing.

Birth Rights.

It had been a short-lived movement just after X-Day. All over the globe, Ones had claimed the exponents weren't human and therefore deserved no human rights. The movement had died, mostly because there were far more exponents than there were Ones, and partly because the world fell apart soon after. It was hard maintaining a hate group when you were facing worldwide starvation, the release of nuclear, biological, and chemical attacks on every continent, and a dearth of shelter for the planet's estimated population of 200 billion humans. But then, that level of population was rather short-lived as well.

"What happened to 1-Patti?" 2-Patti asked.

"She was caught too. Didn't see her again before I escaped."

"Drink." One of the Gregs let 33-Patti sip from his canteen.

"These people beat you?" 23-Patti asked, showing her teeth.

33-Patti nodded.

"Hell no!" 23-Patti said. "What we gonna do about this, 2?"

2-Patti bit the inside of her cheek. "We need to find out all we can about these people. 5-Patti, get the harmony together."

"What about 8?" 5-Patti asked.

"Obviously not her. Just the fourteen we got on the co-op right now. Tell them to pack a ruck. We're going to see the colonel."

23-Patti made a face. "The colonel? What for? That church is in Star. That's where we need to go."

2-Patti shook her head. "The colonel is closer to Star than us. He's probably been trading with those church folk. Maybe he can tell us something we should know before we go out there."

23-Patti folded her arms, looking mulish. She started to speak, but 2-Patti cut her off.

"Fight me on this and I won't take you, 23. I'll leave you here to muck stalls for Daddy Ray."

23-Patti rolled her eyes, but said nothing.

II

The two-lane blacktop between the co-op farm and the city of Anderson was a pitted, overgrown mess impassable by anything but an off-road vehicle. That was fine. Nobody had any gasoline anyway.

"I remember when we could do a twelve-mile ruck carrying fifty pounds and still go for a swim after lunch," 5-Patti said. She, like all the Pattis, carried a thirty-pound load that included everything she would need for a week in the field, and she was panting.

"We used to eat better," 2-Patti said.

"I know that's right," 48-Patti said. "I'd give anything for a mess hall pass right now."

This road had been hemmed in by thick forest on either side broken only now and again by dirt driveways four years ago. Few of those trees remained. A bloated, unchecked population had deforested the entire area, using the wood to either build rude cabins to house exponents or construct walls to keep them out. Only saplings and thorny undergrowth were left.

A village made of a dozen mobile homes set side-by-side and surrounded by twice again as many cabins stood near the road. People tumbled out of the cabins and homes as Patti Harmony passed. Most were children without doubles—kids who had been roughly three years or less when X-Day came. But there were plenty of exponents as well.

Patti Harmony pulled into close formation. There were fourteen of them. Six were armed, but only two had rounds: 2-Patti and 5-Patti. The six put themselves between their harmony and the burgeoning crowd.

"Hey," said a dingy man. He wore jeans covered in red mud, no shoes, and no shirt. "You got any food? We got babies here." He stood on the precipice of a culvert between the road and the makeshift village. He was so dirty, 2-Patti couldn't tell his race.

"No," 2-Patti said.

"I know they ain't," 23-Patti said, looking off at the desolation opposite the crowd. "Well, we can't help 'em 'cause we got our own problems, right?"

2-Patti ignored her harmony mate. Sometimes 23 talked to the air like that. She claimed she came from an alternate dimension and that she could still see and hear the people she had left behind.

She was the only person 2-Patti had ever seen survive the manmade super flu known as Simon Says. The rest had gone insane before the fevers killed them.

Sixteen of the same woman, a skinny thing barely out of her teens, scrambled across the culvert. One of them carried an infant tucked close to her neck.

"We ain't got nothing here," said the mother. "I'm so hungry, I can't make milk. Please, if one of you've got anything—anything at all to eat—please, can I have it?"

"No," 30-Patti said. She was one of the six with a firearm, an old Browning 12-gauge Daddy Ray used for hunting before the world ran out of shells. She raised it, but didn't point it at the mother and her exponents.

"Aw hell," 23-Patti said, rifling through the cargo pockets on the camo shorts she wore. She fished out a couple of carrots and tossed them to mother's exponents.

Though they appeared as frail and starving as their harmony sister, the two that caught the carrots immediately passed them to the mother who crunched into them without hesitation.

"You got more?" asked a skinny black man in a red ball cap surrounded by over twenty copies of himself.

30-Patti pumped the empty shotgun. "Back off!"

2-Patti lifted her M4, her heart in her throat. Killing starving people was not on her agenda today, and she certainly didn't want to add it to her conscience. "Everyone calm down. 5, 26, 30, form up on me. The rest of you, double-time."

The harmony split, the exponents 2-Patti had called making a formation with her across the road while the rest jogged away. The mob of exponents came to a standstill, goggling at Patti Harmony's coordinated movements.

"Listen to me," 2-Patti said, "ten miles back the way we came, there's a farming co-op. We take only those willing to work. We can't shelter you all, but if you're willing to weed, plant, muck out animal stalls, there's a chance you'll eat. Tell them Patti sent you."

Most of the crowd stood silent, sullen, but the skinny mother nodded. "We'll go."

"Yeah, we will," said one of her exponents. "Thank you."

2-Patti and the others backed away until they were a safe distance from the crowd, then turned and hoofed it after the rest of the harmony. Behind them the baby wailed.

III

An old, faded pre-X-Day sign marked the boundary of Anderson County, SC. It had once been green, but time and weather had eroded all but a few flakes of its original color. 2-Patti could just make out the words: Welcome to Anderson, the Electric City. Someone had spray painted a new message beneath the old: Exponent Rights! Origin Does Not Equal Ownership.

"I know that's right," 23-Patti said as she passed the sign.

"You hear something?" 26-Patti asked.

"A truck," 23-Patti said.

"Ain't no trucks running anymore," 45-Patti said.

"No." 2-Patti cocked an ear and opened her mouth to enhance the sound. "She's right."

It was an old-world sound: the drone of an engine revved beyond manufacturing specs. It came from the parking lot of an old shopping center with a Bi-Lo grocery store and a mostly demolished bowling alley about an eighth of a mile from where the Pattis stood. Tires screeched and the distinct, more familiar sound of gunfire erupted.

"Let's go," 2-Patti shouted.

They launched into a jog, alert for ambush, and reached the store while the shooting was still going on. They lined up against the store's wall. 2-Patti risked a peek.

Two trucks and a panel van stood broadside to the store's ruined facade. Someone had stenciled the words *Free State Pendleton* on the side of the van. Gunmen—they were all men—in the truck beds and on either side of the van were firing into the store with an assortment of assault and hunting rifles. The acrid tang of gunpowder flavored the air.

Defenders in the store were returning fire but to little effect. Most of their shots pinged off the parking lot's old asphalt.

"Can't see who's inside," 2-Patti said, "but I'm pretty sure they're with the colonel."

"'Course they are," 23-Patti said, rolling her eyes. The milky one moved slower than the brown. "Who else has bullets to be fighting the Free Staters?"

"What we gonna do?" 5-Patti asked, looking to 2-Patti. "Whoever's in that Bi-Lo, they're pinned down."

2-Patti gripped the stock of her M4 'til her fingers ached. She was no good at this sort of thing. Clutch decisions were 1-Patti's forte.

"2, you gotta decide, girl," 23-Patti said, not unkindly.

"We don't have much ammo," 2-Patti said, mind racing, ideas forming as she spoke. "But we've got the flank and surprise. Pucker factor is in our favor too. Those boys clearly ain't trained. They're failing the stress shoot portion of this exercise, shooting everywhere but the target."

5-Patti nodded. "We get in a few clean kills, you think they'll hightail it?"

"Yeah." 2-Patti hazarded another glance around the corner, trying to muster her confidence. "31, it's you and me. I'll take out the two guys at the van, you get that stupid bastard standing up in the truck bed like a damn scarecrow. After that, it's open season, but conserve ammo. The rest of you stay hidden."

"Got it, Sarge," 31-Patti said with a grin as she checked the action on her Remington 700. It was a single shot, bolt action .308 hunting rifle. Not the most reliable piece of hardware, but accurate as hell.

"Go!" 2-Patti snugged the M4's butt to her shoulder, muzzle down, and crouch-walked twelve feet to lean on a burned out Honda in the parking lot. She didn't concern herself with 31. The girl had skills.

They fired simultaneously on the first shot, the M4's staple-gun-on-steroids cough harmonizing with the 700's more deep-throated boom. Both shots marked their targets.

The scarecrow in the truck bed jerked and toppled to the parking lot. A hairy, overweight guy next to the van followed suit, 2-Patti's bullet taking him in the jaw.

While 31-Patti had to work the action on her 700, 2-Patti popped off four more shots and made four more kills. The Free Staters stared around in confusion, trying to simultaneously duck and see who was picking them off. 31-Patti took out another sheep from their fold.

"Shit!" screamed a scrawny young Free Stater. He couldn't have been more than twenty. He and three of his doubles scrambled into the panel van. One of them got the engine going while a dozen of his comrades outside yelled at him to stop, calling him a coward.

He wasn't a coward. He was smart. He squealed out of the lot, taking two-thirds of the Free Staters' cover with him.

2-Patti continued firing, squeezing off even bursts, syncing them with her breaths. Free Staters fell like pine cones, taking fire from two sides as the defenders in the store increased their volley.

Another three seconds and the truth finally dawned on the eleven men remaining in the parking lot. They were either going to run or die. Their chance for victory was gone.

One of them, a large white man dressed in camo coveralls, screamed something 2-Patti couldn't make out, and they headed for their trucks. A shot from inside the store dropped another one before they could follow the kid they had called a coward, leaving their dead behind. 31-Patti started to fire at their retreating vehicles, but 2-Patti waved her off.

Five men and three women exited the wrecked storefront. Four of the men were the same tall, lanky white guy with gray hair and dark blue eyes. Each carried a matching Winchester rifle.

"Patty Cake!" said three of the Colonel Andrew Boyds at once. All four jogged to meet 2 and 31-Patti in the lot.

The Pattis assumed a position of attention and rendered a military salute sharp enough to slice bread, which made the colonels laugh. They returned the salute.

"Haven't seen you in three months, Sergeant," one of the colonels said to 2-Patti while the others started talking with her harmony mates.

"Been busy with the wedding," 2-Patti said. She lifted an eyebrow. "Are you 1-Andrew by chance?"

He shook his head with a wry grin. "I'm 52. Sorry we couldn't make the wedding, by the way. As you can see, we've been busy." He waved a hand at the blood, bodies, and tire marks on the asphalt. "Thanks for the assist."

"Anytime," 2-Patti said, though she was feeling some regret at how much ammo that little action had cost her. 1-Patti would have found a way to end the firefight without such expense. "I had no idea the Free Staters had gasoline."

"They've got a stash of Pri-G. I don't think they have much, but they're willing to use it against us. They think my town belongs to them."

2-Patti could understand why. Anderson, South Carolina was one of the only peaceful cities she knew of. And it owed that peace to Colonel Boyd and his harmony. Patti had never served under the colonel in active service, he was a Marine, but she had come to respect his leadership since X-Day.

"So what brings you here?" 52-Andrew asked. "I get the feeling you didn't come to reminisce about old times."

"1-Patti's gone missing."

"Missing how?"

"You heard about that church down in Star-Iva? The one supposed to be growing all sorts of food?"

"Yeah. We've got some trade going with them. Can't say I like it much though."

"Why?" 2-Patti asked.

"I've been hearing things about them—talk of rekindling that Birth Rights nonsense from back at the beginning. You think 1-Patti joined them?"

2-Patti shook her head, keenly aware of her harmony listening to their conversation. "I don't know."

"So why did you come here?" 52-Andrew asked.

"Ain't that a good question," 23-Patti said to the empty air over one shoulder.

"I need to know the layout of the place. What sort of security they got there? How many harmonies? That sort of thing. I could use your help planning what to do."

52-Andrew eyed her for a long moment. Then he motioned for 2-Patti to follow him into the ruined store away from the others. When they were out of earshot, he rounded on her. "Is something wrong with you, soldier?"

"No, sir. I'm just—"

"Sergeant First Class Cook, did you really just ruck march to Anderson when your primary target is miles from here? You're special forces. Is there anything I could tell you about this church that you couldn't have found on your own?"

"Colonel, I—"

52-Andrew held up a hand. "Don't even start with whatever bullshit was about to pour out of your mouth. You think I don't recognize a crisis of confidence when I see one? You're not her, am I right?"

2-Patti's throat constricted the way it always did whenever a superior dressed her down. "No, sir. I'm not her. I'm me."

"Number two. Second best. Is that it?" 52-Andrew asked.

2-Patti shook her head, though a small voice inside whispered that it was true.

"Bull. You think it every minute you're awake. I'm number fifty-two in my harmony. I know how it feels. It's easy to start thinking you're not as good as your One— that you're not real. But you got to stomp that shit right out of your head now, Sergeant. You're about to lead your sisters into an unknown. You can't doubt yourself. You are Patti Cook. You've got everything she's got. You either believe that and make it true, or you wither away into a shell of yourself. Which is it?"

"She's better at—"

"Bullshit. Step up, Sergeant."

2-Patti swallowed. Her throat felt suddenly dry. "I will, sir."

"You'd better. Now, I can't do a lot to help you. My resources are strapped keeping this town safe. But I'll replace the ammo you spent saving us, and I think we can spare you a couple of radios. After that, you need to get the hell out of my town and get your ass on task." 52-Andrew said this without rancor. He even spared 2-Patti a slight grin when she looked up.

"I will, sir."

IV

Patti Harmony reached the outskirts of Starr, South Carolina at 0930 the next morning. Like most towns in the deep south after X-Day, Starr was rural, impoverished to the point of daily death tolls, and starving. Indolent harmonies gathered outside their makeshift homes in abandoned gas stations and storefronts to watch the Pattis. Many of the women had squalling infants in their arms or small kids chasing about. 2-Patti shook her head at that. How anyone could bring a child into this world was beyond her.

They reached a widened stretch of asphalt where SC HWY 81 merged into Starr's main road, Stones Throw Avenue. 2-Patti lifted a fist to call a halt.

"Okay, we're going to split up," she said. "I want four of you with me—not you, 23, I'm sorry."

23-Patti put her hands on her hips. "Don't be leaving me out, 2."

"If this is leaving you out then I'm doing it to nearly everybody," 2-Patti said. "26, 45, 60, and 31 you're with me. The rest are in reserve. Make camp nearby and be listening for my signal. If things go south for us with this church, I'll radio."

"You sure about this?" 34-Patti asked. "Maybe we should all go—power in numbers and all."

"No. I'm not sure about any of this, but I know I'll want backup if things go pear-shaped. Better if ya'll are a surprise."

"I know, Mama, but she don't listen to me," 23-Patti said loud enough for everybody to hear.

2-Patti rolled her eyes. "Just say whatever you're gonna say, 23."

"It ain't me!" 23-Patti looked offended. "It's Mama-Gloria from my dimension."

"Fine. What does Mama-Gloria from the 23rd dimension have to say about my plan?"

"She say, 'Don't these church people already know about all of us since they got 1-Patti and the others?'"

"Maybe," 2-Patti said. "But we don't know what we don't know, right? That's the oldest problem for any army. Maybe our sisters told them about us, and maybe they didn't. Either way, I think we're better off going into the unknown with something in reserve."

23-Patti stared off into space for a moment, nodding. "Mama say, 'You the sergeant, and maybe you know more,' but she also say, 'You crazy for not taking 23 with you.' Now that wasn't me, that was Mama-Gloria."

2-Patti smiled and hugged 23. "I know you want to go to protect me, but you can do that better as backup. All right?"

23-Patti nodded.

The harmony split, and 2-Patti led her four sisters into the town proper, which was little more than a weedy wide spot in the road.

A crowd of children—there must have been fifty of them, dressed in rags and so caked with dirt and grime they looked like war refugees—abandoned their play in the street to follow.

"Who are you?" asked a little blonde girl.

"You a soldier?" asked a dark-haired boy wearing a Spider-Man pajama top two sizes too small.

Most of the children bore those two faces. They were likely brother and sister from the look of them. Their exponents were just as full of questions. It was like rolling into Baghdad when all the kids would come dancing out of alleyways begging for candy and patting you with their little hands.

"We don't have anything," 30-Patti and 31-Patti said at the same time.

"Is there a church around here? One that's been growing a lot of food?" 2-Patti asked.

"Oh, yeah, them cult people." The blonde girl gave 2-Patti a confiding smirk.

One of the boys shushed her. "We ain't supposed to talk about them, Rubyanne. Mama said so."

Several of the Rubyannes shrugged while others gave the boy a roll of their eyes. Their movements were so coordinated, it made 2-Patti smile. These kids probably couldn't remember much of the world without doubles. Communication like this was second nature to them.

"Mama does say they're a cult," confided the Rubyanne speaking with 2-Patti. "But they got food, so everybody trades with 'em."

"Where's their church?"

The nearest Rubyanne pointed along Stones Throw Ave. "Straight that way and then left at Smith McGee Road. You can't miss it. They got a big white wall and two huge buildings and lots of people out working in the fields all dressed like pilgrims."

"Thank you. Are you 1-Rubyanne?"

The little girl shrugged. "I dunno."

"We lost track," said one of her doubles.

29-Patti raised her eyebrows at that.

"I guess kids aren't so concerned about who's who," 2-Patti said. She refrained from adding, *Maybe adults could learn something from that.*

V

The church was indeed surrounded by a stone wall just as Rubyanne had promised. It was whitewashed and stood ten feet high. Rusty razor wire snaked along its top.

"We're not getting over that without trouble," 48-Patti said.

"And not without knowing what's on the other side," 2-Patti said.

Hundreds of men and women, many of them duplicates of one another, worked in a field opposite the wall, tilling the land with hoes and shovels. Rubyanne proved right again. These farmhands were dressed conservatively, but not like pilgrims, more like Amish or plain folk. The men wore black pants and vests with colored button-up shirts. Most had long beards and shaggy hair. The women wore long skirts of gray, blue, or black. And not one was bareheaded—they all wore bonnets that tied under their chins to cover their hair.

"You think they're slaves?" 26-Patti whispered to 2.

2-Patti shook her head. "Probably not. I don't see anybody watching them. If they're slaves, where're the overseers?"

"I think we might be about to find out," 34-Patti said.

A small crowd, maybe 150 to 200 people, had gathered in front of a swing arm gate set into the wall. They weren't dressed like the farmers, but wore the usual assortment of post-X fashions: worn blue jeans, tennis shoes that had seen too many miles, shirts streaked with stains, and hats to deflect the sun. They stank of sour sweat—a stench every Patti knew.

"This the revival meeting?" 45-Patti asked a black woman who looked to be in her sixties.

Three of her turned to smile and say, "Yeah, honey."

"You'll have to check your weapons," said a burly man dressed like the farmers across the street. He and one of his harmony mates strolled along the line with several others, pushing wheelbarrows full of guns, knives, chains, and even a few rocks.

All the Pattis looked to 2-Patti at this news.

"We get them back?" 2-Patti asked.

The man nodded. One of his doubles, who bore a deep scar down his left cheek that his twin didn't have, said, "Yes. We'll give you chit for it."

A military guy, then. That didn't mean 2-Patti could trust him, or any of his ilk, but it eased her mind. Slightly.

"Okay," 2-Patti said. She put on a brave face, and handed the scarred man her M4. He passed her back a handwritten note with its make and serial number printed in blocky letters. At 2-Patti's example, the other Pattis gave up their few guns and many knives.

A band started to play from somewhere behind the wall, picking out a twangy version of Amazing Grace with guitars and banjos.

"Oh, it's starting!" said one of the old women.

Someone opened the gate from the inside to reveal an acre of green grass that rolled up to a white, three story building. The place was ostentatious. It didn't belong in Starr, that was certain. It looked like someone had either copied an old world European cathedral, or moved an original one here brick-by-brick. Honest to God castle turrets stood at each of its four corners with crenelated tops and small stained glass windows set into their stones.

"Wow," 64-Patti said. "They're really going for awe factor here, aren't they?"

"I guess this is their temple," 2-Patti said.

Her harmony nodded their heads.

"Looks like they got power too," 31-Patti said, pointing to a row of windmills that dominated several acres of the walled-in property.

"You can't pump out good gospel music without an amp," 29-Patti said.

One of the old women doubles within earshot gave her a dirty look and 2-Patti signaled for her harmony to be silent. They didn't need any more complications than they already had.

A stage stood in front of the temple. It had all the trappings of a pre-X concert with it's multi-colored lights set into the roof, microphones on stands, and speakers as tall as Patti. A large, enclosed tent, nearly the size of a big top at a pre-X circus, stood next to the stage. Some in the crowd headed toward it, but were shooed away by a covey of conservatively dressed women.

"This way, folks," said one black woman dressed in a long blue skirt and head covering.

"Sorry, we don't have any chairs," said another of her.

"You won't miss them," said a third. "You'll be having too much fun!"

Patty Harmony stuck together, as did most of the harmonies in the crowd. They ended up relatively close to the stage, standing with the woman who had spoken to them outside.

"This your first time coming here?" asked one of the old woman's exponents.

2-Patti nodded.

"They got a good message and a good preacher. We just aren't sure we're ready for all he's asking of us."

"What do you mean—" 2-Patti started to ask, but was cut off when a tall, well-muscled white man took the stage and the crowd burst into enthusiastic applause.

He wore a fine suit. It was steel gray with a crease down each leg. His gold tie complimented his watch and rings. His shoes were polished, his teeth were white, and he looked like he had been eating well.

60-Patti leaned and whispered in 2-Patti's ear, "Now that's a preacher."

"How y'all doing?" he asked in a voice that was deep and rich.

The crowd again exploded in raucous cheers and applause.

He smiled and pulled the main microphone from its stand. "For y'all that don't know me, my name's Reverend Phillip Sligh."

The crowd tried to cheer again, but Sligh held up his hands. "Y'all come here for a revival meeting, but I'm here to tell you this ain't about revival, it's about survival, brothers and sisters."

A chorus of "Amen!" and "Preach it, brother!" rang from the crowd.

"Old ways are what got us into this mess. Old ways were sin and lasciviousness. I'm telling you all now, the exponents, as the great minds of our day call them, are not evil as some have preached. But they are a curse put upon this world by the everliving God—a curse that nevertheless brings with it a message of hope and gladness for the eternities.

"Now, some of you might already have heard the good news. Maybe some folks told you that the Church of the

Sanctified One was a cult—that we're spreading lies and making slaves of people."

A few in the crowd—2-Patti noted with interest that they were dressed ultra-conservatively—laughed at this, or shouted, "Ain't true," or "Lies!"

"If devotion to the one everliving, everloving, everlasting God in heaven is a lie, then make me a slave today, brothers and sisters!" Sligh shouted the words, making them ring across the crowd. He turned then and waved his hand at the entrace to the tent.

A line of Reverend Phillip Sligh's exponents marched onto the stage. Each wore the same plaid shirt with plain black pants and work boots. They walked quickly, forming up behind their double with the microphone, but it still took nearly a minute for them to all assemble. The crowd began to murmur and makes sounds of surprise as the seconds passed and the trickle of Slighs continued. The last to appear brought his well-dressed double on the stage a bottle of water.

"Thank you, 64," Sligh said.

"Did you count them?" 45-Patti whispered. "There's 64 of them."

2-Patti had counted, but was doubting her tally. "That's not possible. Nobody has a perfect 64." Colonel Boyd had the most complete harmony she had ever seen, and his harmony boasted only about fifty exponents.

Sligh let the moment last a little longer, taking a slow sip of water. He put the bottle down next to his mic stand, and when he turned back to the crowd, he had assumed a grave expression. "You see, brothers and sisters, I am a blessed man. God has sheltered my harmony with His own hand from the breaking of mankind so that we can bring you His new message—His new dispensation. Forget what you've been told about me and our church. Let God himself explain the hurt and heartache and sacrifice you've been living through lo these last four years."

"You've all heard about the war in heaven. You know that the souls who fought against our Father God were sent to the fiery pit with their foul master, Satan. And that the good souls who remained valiant sons and daughters were allowed to come down to this Earth to be tried. Those are the Ones, brothers and sisters. Some of you are Ones. Most of you are not. Now, don't despair, thinking I've tricked you somehow—that I'm against exponents. Brothers and sisters, some of my dearest friends are exponents!"

Sligh's army of doubles laughed on cue, and 2-Patti felt her stomach go tight. No matter what he said, she was certain it wasn't going to be equality for exponents, not with him standing there in his thousand dollar suit and Rolex watch.

"There has been a second war in heaven, y'all," Sligh said. "A second war in which the forces of the evil one connived and wrangled many good souls to rail against our Father which art in heaven. Now I don't know the minds of demons. I can't think how they imagined they would overthrow the architect of the universe, and they didn't. God's forces bested them four years ago. The evil souls who came against our Father were banished back to hell fire. But those souls who had served God valiantly in the first war, only to turn traitor during this second conflict, begged for mercy. God, being ever beneficent, decided to make an example of these souls, both to the living and the dead. He sent them here not as individuals, for they did not deserve such in his estimation. Instead, they became copies of those who had gone before."

Another round of murmuring broke out in the crowd, this time much less pleased sounding than before.

"I knew it," 2-Patti said.

"I know some of you Ones, your exponents won't hear of serving. They say they're people just like you, and to that I say, it's true. It's true they are people, they deserve dignity. But what of their souls, brothers and sisters? They fought against the Most High and lost. They were sent here as copies of copies as punishment for that sin! To serve is to live everlasting life. You exponents who have taken your rightful place, I bless you in the name of Jesus, for you have chosen the hard path—the hard way! And you will be returned to your Father in heaven triumph amongst the brothers or sisters of your harmony, a peer and an equal in the kingdom come."

"You buying this crap, 2?" 64-Patti asked.

"Hello no," 2-Patti said. She had to purposefully stop grinding her teeth as the preacher continued. "I've heard enough. Let's see if we can scout around a little. Maybe one of us will spot 1-Patti."

"Uh, 2," 48-Patti said, pointing a shaking finger at the stage.

Apparently, Sligh had called for testimonies from members of his ridiculous church while 2-Patti wasn't listening. 1-Patti, dressed like an Amish woman, exited the tent with a radiant smile creasing her dark cheeks. She strode to Sligh's side with purpose, and he handed her the microphone.

"Hello, my name's Patti Cook." She focused her gaze on her harmony mates. "Pattis. I knew you'd come. Welcome home."

A commotion in the crowd caught 2-Patti's attention. Dozens of church members in their plain attire were converging on Patti Harmony. A large black man caught

45-Patti by the arm. She tried to resist, but three of his doubles got hands on her.

Some in the crowd protested, but none offered help. They spread out in a circle to watch the spectacle.

"Patti!" shouted 2-Patti. "Why are you doing this? What have they done?"

"Don't resist them," 1-Patti said into the microphone. "No one's going to hurt you. We just need to talk."

An average-sized white guy and two of his doubles surrounded 2-Patti. She didn't give them time to formulate a plan. She kicked the one in front of her in the knee and spun him bodily into the others. Then she keyed the radio at her throat. "The Jaybird sings!"

Static crackled in her ear as she dodged the grasp of a small woman, only to have a set of triplets, each the size of a small boulder, lift her bodily from the ground. The men were too strong for her to mount any sort of effective defense. It was like she was a two-year-old resisting a parent.

Desperately, she keyed the radio a second time. "Pattis! The Jaybird sings!"

The sound of 2-Patti's voice, tinny and static filled, erupted from somewhere nearby. Even as she struggled in vain to resist the triplets, 2-Patti searched the crowd until her gaze found her own eyes staring back.

At least fifty cultists stood in a semi-circle off to one side of the stage, pointing an assortment of rifles and handguns at the exponents 2-Patti had left in the woods. Nearly all of Patti Harmony was there except for one or two—it was hard to tell even for her. 23-Patti must have run off. She was probably scared out of her mind, what was left of it right now. Poor thing.

"Stop fighting," 2-Patti said to the rest of her sisters. They too had seen the hostages. Most had already quit, but at 2-Patti's order, the rest fell still.

"This is for the best, Patti," 1-Patti said from the stage. "We're going to be happy. You'll see."

VI

"Why are you doing this?" 2-Patti struggled against the three burly men hustling her toward the temple. She could just see 1-Patti behind her, strolling with 1-Phillip at her side.

"That's my 2," 1-Patti said to 1-Phillip.

1-Phillip pointed at the temple doors. His men separated Patti Harmony, 2-Patti's abductors hauling her inside while scores of other cultists dragged the other Pattis toward a long row of trailers—a real eyesore— behind the temple.

The temple smelled like sawdust and new paint. Electric lights burned overhead, throwing an unnatural glow over gilded portraits of Jesus and saints and depictions of bible stories hanging in the vestibule. The men carried 2-Patti up a flight of stairs that opened into a hallway on the second floor. Their footfalls echoed in the dim corridor.

They passed several doorways with small, shatterproof windows set at eye level. 2-Patti thought she glimpsed one of her harmony mates through one of the windows, but couldn't be certain. They had moved on before she got a good look.

The men shoved Patti into a cell five doors down and on the right. They forced her into a chair that looked like it belonged in a dentist's office. One of the doubles held her still while two of them secured 2-Patti's wrists and ankles with leather straps.

2-Patti kept calm. She wanted answers. She wasn't going to get them if she fought.

1-Patti eyed her, no doubt surmising her exponent's thoughts without effort.

Two white women dressed in floral-patterned scrubs entered the room. One carried what 2-Patti at first took for a small pistol in one hand. But no, it was some sort of medical device. It was brown and white, with a hand grip on one end and a flared tip. A light glowed green on one side of the thing.

The second woman, twin to the first, pulled a syringe and several empty vials from a scrubs pocket.

2-Patti's heart sped up. She swallowed.

"Shall I, Phillip?" asked the twin with the gun.

1-Phillip nodded gravely.

The nurse rolled 2-Patti's sleeve up to expose her biceps.

"What is this?" 2-Patti asked 1-Patti. She could no longer fight the feelings of betrayal pervading her emotions.

"It's a test," 1-Phillip said, "to determine the probability that you are the One from your harmony."

"You think 1-Patti lied to you?"

"We can never be too sure," 1-Phillip said. "A lot of exponents would like to be the One. And sometimes, with all the confusion in this fallen world, people forget their rightful number. It's understandable. You share your original's memories, after all."

The nurse pressed the gun's tip against 2-Patti's exposed skin and pulled the trigger. There followed a static burp, a sting of pain, and the odor of burnt flesh.

2-Patti clenched her teeth.

"Sorry," the nurse said. "It cauterizes after taking the sample. Don't worry, though, it won't leave a scar."

"I thought there was no way to tell us apart," 2-Patti said, still looking at 1-Patti.

1-Phillip grinned, probably at the way 2-Patti refused to look at him. "A handful of firms scrambled to solve the problem right before the great collapse. That one is called a Divisor. It's a prototype created by Clarke Glaxor and Kline, the pharmaceutical lab. It's quite reliable. I've tested it against my own harmony several times."

The second nurse tied a thick rubber band about 2-Patti's upper arm and proceeded to search for a vein.

"If it works so well, why do you need to draw blood?"

"The Divisor isn't perfect. We have a second means of determining your place with a blood sample, but it takes a few days to complete."

The second nurse swabbed 2-Patti's inner elbow with a musty smelling suave then pushed the needled into her vein. Blood bubbled up into its vial, driven hard by her speeding heart.

"This is all lies," 2-Patti said to her original. "You know I'm not an exponents rights nut, but we're people just like you. We're equal."

"I know you are," 1-Patti said, the sincerity on her face and in her voice genuine and sad. "And you will be equal in the eternities."

The nurse switched out vials on the syringe, sending a stinging tingle of pain up 2-Patti's arm.

"But just not here and now?" 2-Patti said, grimacing.

"Exponents must pay a price in servitude for their actions in the second heavenly war," 1-Phillip said, his eyes suddenly full of fervor.

"Bullshit," 2-Patti said. "Who the hell are you, anyway? You made this shit up and now you've got your own harmony believing it, and all these gullible people. It's insane."

"It's the gospel," 1-Patti said, slowly shaking her head with pity.

The machine in the first nurse's hands beeped. She peered at a small screen on its back end for a second, then smiled. "This is almost definitely one of Patti's exponents. Probability is in the high nineties."

"How does it tell that?" 2-Patti asked.

"The Divisor measures the telomeres in your DNA," said one nurse.

"They're little end caps on the strands," said the other.

"The older you are, the shorter your telomere caps. Exponents have abnormally long ones. Makes it easy to tell them apart from originals," said the first.

"Good," 1-Phillip said with a smile. "Then we know we're dealing with 2-Patti after all."

A look of relief passed over 1-Patti's features.

"You were worried we had gotten mixed up somewhere along the way," 2-Patti said. "Afraid you might be the one made a slave?"

1-Phillip shook his head, his lips turned down in mild reproof. "No one on church premises is a slave, Patti. The exponents here serve willingly, because they share faith in the gospel. "I know you find that hard to understand right now. But I think you'll come around. Your One has."

"My *One* has lost her mind. And what you're doing here is wrong."

"You witnessed my harmony," 1-Phillip said. "We are a perfect 64."

"So?"

"How can you believe that possible outside of divine intervention? We made it through the plagues, wars, and civil unrest of the last four years unscathed. Have you ever heard of another harmony to have done that? God protected us for His grand purpose."

"You hid somewhere like a bunch of cowards. Probably refused to help anyone but yourselves the whole time."

1-Phillip shook his head slowly, a beautific smile on his face—the indulgent father suffering his daughter's tirade with good humor and patience. He stepped forward to gently place his hand on 2-Patti's cheek. "I know you, Patti, because I know your One. She is tough as old hickory, and dangerous in ways I and my harmony can't even imagine. But she's also kind and contemplative—the sort who will put herself in danger to protect a co-op of farmers whom she could have ruled had she but wished it. She, and her harmony, are just what the Church of the Anointed One need right now— just what I need right now. 1-Patti will be my general. She will run my armies, command the Church's foot soldiers. And you will be her adjunct. Together, we will feed and protect the masses. Isn't that exactly what you're trying to do already? Join with us, and we will reunite the world under our banner."

2-Patti gritted her teeth through Phillip's sermon. Rage boiled inside her. This man was a charlatan. How could 1-Patti not see that? Was she so enamored with the idea of command that the possibility was blinding her? Maybe they really were different after all. 2-Patti couldn't imagine ever joining this man. He would never have her loyalty.

Giving him no warning, 2-Patti jerked her head to the side and bit into 1-Phillip's thumb. She didn't stint, but ground her teeth, jerking her head side-to-side. She tasted blood.

1-Phillip screamed. He struggled to free his hand while his stunned guards looked on in horror, seemingly too shocked to react for a several seconds.

Then a hard fist connected with the side of 2-Patti's head. She lost consciousness for maybe half a second, blotches of swirling black and purple threatening to swallow her vision. When she came to, 1-Phillip stood cradling his bloodied hand against his expensive suit coat, while 1-Patti held 2-Patti's head back by the hair, fist raised to deliver another blow.

"Goddamn that bitch!" 1-Phillip roared.

"You don't touch him," 1-Patti said, wrenching 2-Patti's hair with each syllable. "You don't deserve to touch him!"

Despite the physical pain, despite the feeling of utter betrayal that made her want to curl into a ball and wither away like a grape, and despite the fear she was too proud to admit was turning her insides into jelly, 2-Patti smiled. She could taste blood on her teeth—Phillip's blood—and she hoped it showed. "Go to hell, sister."

VII

They did a good job of chaining her up. Padded leather cuffs kept 2-Patti's arms above her head with just enough slack so that she could either stand or hang, but never sit. A matching set of manacles bound her ankles. They kept her in place, unable to do more than shift her weight from one painfully aching leg to the other.

Was 1-Patti behind the arrangement? Maybe. 1-Phillip, or perhaps some of his flunkies, might have designed it, but this sort of enhanced interrogation device had devious Ranger written all over it.

2-Patti would have thought of it.

She heaved a sigh, rolling her shoulders to coax some blood flow. Her hands had gone from pins and needles to severe pain hours ago with only a brief, and again painful, reprieve. Now they were lifeless things, numb as two dead fish hanging on hooks.

She couldn't tell the time, which was frustrating. The room had no windows nor clocks. The walls were smooth and white. 1-Phillip had even ordered his guards to remove the chair where the nurse had drawn 2-Patti's blood, making the most interesting thing in the place its bland carpet decorated in squares of varying shades of tan.

The room was silent except for the rasp of 2-Patti's breathing and the chain rattling when she moved. It had been a long time since she had experienced silence. That was a rare commodity in a world so filled with people.

2-Patti hated it.

She could hear her heart beating, and the hollow gurgling in her stomach. She hadn't eaten since before she arrived at the compound. That too was part of the torture. No sleep, no food, no dignity.

The cultists had allowed her to use the toilet once. Six women, all from the same harmony, had stripped her clothes away and hustled her down the hall, naked save for the chains, to a small lavatory. They had watched her do her business then hustled her back. Her door guards, the three burly guys who had carried her here, had gotten an eyeful. The women had drawn a near see-through shift over 2-Patti's head before chaining her back to the wall.

The worst part was understanding what was happening and remaining powerless to change it. Beyond the discomfort, the pain, the psychological aspects, there laid the mindfulness. 2-Patti could know what was happening to her—she had seen it happen to detainees back in Afghanistan—but that knowledge hardly made a difference. Her body reacted like any other body in this situation, and that included her brain. She was strong now, but eventually she would break—was already breaking.

2-Patti let her body hang from the wrist straps for a few seconds, knees bent, toes on the floor, giving her hips and back a short-lived reprieve from holding her up. Her shoulders screamed in pain. Her arms and hands felt nothing, which was probably worse. A cramp flared in her hip. She got her feet back on the floor, but could do nothing to work out the clenching muscle. She groaned.

As if in answer, 2-Patti heard a sound outside her door. Several sounds, really. First came a thump, followed by the echo of scuttling feet, a deep-throated cry of alarm or anger, then several more thumps.

2-Patti's cell door swung open and 23-Patti sauntered inside wearing a long ocher robe that could have been a dress except it was split down the middle to reveal her regular clothes beneath. She carried a length of wood in one hand and a Colt .45 in the other.

"Rangers, lead the way," 23-Patti said, her mismatched eyes sparkling. She flourished her stick, which 2-Patti suddenly realized was a policeman's club, once around her wrist like a cheerleader's baton then shoved it into the belt of her camo booty shorts. "Hi, sis. Miss me?"

2-Patti couldn't smile. She was in too much pain. But she shook with relief at seeing her harmony mate.

5-Patti entered the door behind 23. She gasped when she saw 2-Patti and hurried over with a set of keys she must have pilfered from the guards outside.

2-Patti groaned when they helped her drop her arms. They eased her to the floor, 5-Patti bracing her so that she wouldn't crack her head open.

23-Patti stood next to the cell door, humming to herself, alternately peeking out and stealing glances at 2-Patti.

"I'm sorry we didn't get here faster," 5-Patti whispered. She fished a squeeze bottle from the pack she wore and gave 2-Patti a sip.

"How?" 2-Patti croaked. She hadn't realized just how dry and sore her throat felt.

"23," 5-Patti said, nodding at their harmony mate. "She hauled me off into the woods when those cultists came to round us up. We kept hidden until it was clear. We stole some clothes from a line and walked in the front gate dressed all Polly Pilgrim. Nobody said a thing to us."

"Believe me, nobody questions dirt," 23-Patti said. "We look like nothing, then we ain't worth talking to."

"And you just walked in here?" 2-Patti asked.

5-Patti shook her head. "It wasn't that easy. We had to do some sneaking to get in this place, but these people have shoddy security."

"They wasn't nobody guarding the rooms downstairs," 23-Patti said. "They had three guards on this hall, but didn't none of them know how to fight. They all laying out in the hallway right now. If one moves, I'll bop him."

"Where are 1-Patti and the others?" 5-Patti asked. She gave 2-Patti another drink.

"1-Patti's aligned herself with these freaks," 2-Patti said. "I think some of the others are locked in cells on this floor."

"1-Patti's part of this?"

Some feeling was coming back into 2-Patti's arms and hands. They hurt like hell, and she had no fine motor skills whatsoever, but she could move them a bit. That was a start. "Yes, but we'll talk about it later. Help me up."

2-Patti couldn't make a fist, and she required 5-Patti's help just to walk, but together the three of them exited the room.

23-Patti leveled her Colt on the nearest guard who was starting to rouse. "Shoot him?"

2-Patti shook her head. "No. We're not murdering anybody."

23-Patti frowned. She looked put out.

"The sound will draw attention," 2-Patti said.

"Oh. That's true," 23-Patti said. She squatted in front of the big man who had just opened his eyes. "You move and I'll beat you to death with my nightstick. That won't make enough noise to be heard outside."

The man, who had obviously already seen the nasty end of 23-Patti's club as evidenced by several cuts and nascent purple bruises on his face, nodded and remained still.

5-Patti began opening cell doors. It was slow going. The things had old-fashioned key locks, forcing her to try key after key until she struck pay dirt.

None of the other Pattis had been tortured like 2-Patti. The cultists had dressed them in shifts, given them little food and water, and no creature comforts, not even cots to sleep on, but none wore chains. So that was to the good.

The reunion was truncated. 2-Patti allowed for, and shared in, a few hugs and even some tears, but the harmony wasn't safe here. Every sound they made put her nerves on edge.

She took a quick head count to busy her mind. They were ten mostly unarmed, hungry, and hurting women. They faced an unknown number of enemy zealots, at least one of whom was the OG Patti Cook, and they were miles from home.

"That's enough, ladies," she said. The harmony grew still, and 2-Patti felt suddenly uncomfortable under their scrutiny. What would 1-Patti do in this situation. Would she—

2-Patti squashed the thought. She refused to fall back on her old ways of thinking. What would 1-Patti do? She would turn against her own harmony to follow some whack job of a cult leader who thought the bulk of humans alive today should be slaves.

Screw that.

"Okay. Here's what we're going to do."

VIII

The temple was empty and only lightly guarded on the outside. 2-Patti outlined a search plan, splitting her harmony by twos. They found what she wanted on the first floor in a set of offices built behind the temple's vainglorious east wall. One of the rooms was filled to the gilded ceiling with medical supplies, including a crash cart, hundreds of syringes and small boxes of medicines with names the Pattis couldn't pronounce, and other med tech.

"They must have raided a hospital early on," 64-Patti said.

"Or a pharmacy," 33-Patti said.

2-Patti ignored them. Her mind was reeling with possibilities. Part of her wanted to strip this place clean. They had no doctors back on the co-op, but Cecelia Flint had been a Physician's Assistant for twenty years leading up to X-Day. Her harmony would know what to do with this stuff. But stealing it meant taking it away from all the people living here. Just because they were following a cult leader didn't mean they deserved to be harmed.

"You thinking we should take it?" 27-Patti asked.

The question almost cracked 2-Patti's resolve. She nearly gave her harmony mates the go-ahead to take all they could carry. It would be that easy. One domino tumbles and the whole line goes down.

She drew a deep breath, and shook her head. "No. We've got no reason to harm these people."

"How about them holding us prisoner?" 13-Patti asked.

"And torturing you," 18-Patti said.

2-Patti slipped a small, brown satchel from a peg on the wall. The DNA testing gun, 1-Phillip had called it the Divisor, lay snug inside. It was a near priceless object in this ruined world.

She slipped the satchel over one shoulder. "No. We're taking what we came for and getting back to the co-op."

"Now all we need is a Phillip," 23-Patti said, her lips curled at the edges in a malicious little grin.

2-Patti grinned right back. "Let's go find one."

IX

The temple guards were big and armed, but stupid and blind. Patti Harmony took out all five inside two minutes. They were all from one harmony, a musclebound Chicano with a jagged scar under his right eye. He must have thought it made him look tough, but it didn't do a thing for his abilities. The Pattis tied the five together using their own flannel shirts and locked them in a temple cell. They managed it without a shot fired.

"Now what?" 5-Patti asked. She stood at the temple entrance, a Kalashnikov resting on one shoulder.

"Take everyone but 23—check out those trailers behind this building," 2-Patti said. "I have a feeling the rest of our harmony's there, and probably a lot more to boot. If the patrols here are any indication, you shouldn't have any trouble. Bring any who can fight. If there are any casualties, we'll deal with them later."

The others wanted to protest, but 2-Patti cut them off.

"We need numbers if we're going to win free of this place. You've got your orders," she said, grinning to show it was a half a joke. "Lead the way."

X

The revival was once again in full swing. Amplified organ music reverberated around the compound. 2-Patti reconnoitered the stage from the leeward side of the temple, crouching in its shadow. 23-Patti squatted next to her, humming to herself and periodically whispering to someone who wasn't there.

Phillip's Harmony had already made their entrance. They stood behind the preacher in eight uniform rows on the stage while he harangued an audience of hundreds. Dozens of armed guards stood in front of the stage with others patrolling the outskirts.

"Here they come," 23-Patti whispered.

Their harmony came around the opposite side of the temple, 5-Patti in the lead. Her face was grim, but her eyes were bright.

"Is that everyone?" 2-Patti asked. Dozens of her were still streaming into view accompanied by exponents from a dozen other harmonies. They all looked starved and tired, their hair disheveled, their skin mottled with bruises. Each wore a thin shift, even the men.

"All of ours," 5-Patti said. "Some of the others were dead."

2-Patti cursed. "You explained the plan to them? Not everyone has to go. They can stay here if they want, or maybe head out if they think it's safe."

"I explained it. They're all in."

"Okay," 2-Patti said, nodding. "Let's do this."

XI

No one was more surprised than 23-Patti when 2-Patti handed her the Kalashnikov rifle. Her brown eyes went round as tennis balls.

"Stay near me," 2-Patti said. "I won't be able to handle a weapon for what I'm about to do."

"Yes, Sergeant," 23-Patti said, grinning. She cut her mismatched eyes to one side, looking off at nothing. "She trust me. I know. I know. Maybe she just desperate and needing backup, but she didn't ask 5-Patti, did she? She ask me—23!"

It felt good having her harmony around her. 2-Patti motioned for them to spread out on either flank. They did so with aplomb, shepherding the other exponents they had rescued to follow.

1-Phillip, who had been exhorting his parishioners to worship their Ones for the security of their everlasting souls, sputtered to a stop. "Guards! We have a situation!"

The crowd turned to face 2-Patti. She would not quell before them or before Phillip's bumbling guards who were trying, and mostly failing, to work their way through the people.

2-Patti pulled the Divisor from its case and held it aloft. It was clear the guards recognized it. Most of them stopped moving immediately. The crowd parted before her, egged on by armed versions of herself pushing them back, if not gently than with less force than they could have employed. She and 23-Patti approached the stage.

"You give that to my guards," 1-Phillip said. "You don't deserve to touch it, exponent."

"If one of your people even comes near me, this thing's going in the air. How many shots you think it will take my harmony to pulverize it?" 2-Patti asked.

1-Patti appeared from the nearby tent to climb the stage steps. She stood next to 1-Phillip, her eyes round with anger. "What the hell are you doing?"

2-Patti hesitated. She had always deferred to her original. The sight of 1-Patti's shock and anger gave her pause. But no. What was going on here wasn't right. And no matter how much it hurt to face the truth, 1-Patti was part of it all.

"What are we doing?" 2-Patti said, finding strength as she spoke. "The right thing!" She turned slowly, facing the crowd. "This man and his people tortured me and my harmony, and many other harmonies, all because we're exponents who refuse to worship our One. This device I'm holding can tell the difference between Ones and exponents. He's using it to divide harmonies and create slaves!"

Some in the crowd started to murmur. A couple of the guards and devout cultists raised voices of descent, but the Pattis shouted them down.

1-Philip drowned them all out with his amplified voice. "Lies. This woman was never tortured. No one was. I have simply tried my best, put forth my sincerest hand of friendship and guidance, to show her the way God would have her go." He lifted his hand over his head as if testifying in court.

23-Patti leaned closer to 2-Patti. "My Mama-Gloria say, 'Check out that preacher's hand—ain't no bite mark there.' She say the one you bit standing three Phillips from the right. You see that?"

2-Patti felt her eyes go round. 23-Patti was right. The Phillip holding the mike had unblemished hands. He wasn't 1-Phillip, or maybe he was. Either way, the one she had bitten stood just where 23-Patti said.

"They're taking turns," 2-Patti said.

23-Patti nodded. "King for a day."

"You're not a One!" 2-Patti shouted at Phillip.

The Phillip with the mike kept his composure, but his gaze flitted momentarily to the man 2-Patti had bitten. That one put his hands behind his back.

2-Patti turned to the crowd. "These men are lying to you! The one in front, he's not 1-Phillip. They're taking turns leading this cult."

The crowd looked about, gazing from 2-Patti to the Phillips and back. Even a few of Phillip's guards looked unsure.

"Get that woman out of here," shouted the Phillip with the mike. "She is disrupting a solemn meeting of God's chosen!"

"If you're a One, then you won't mind taking your own test," 2-Patti shouted, holding up the Divisor.

"I've no need to take it, Jezebel. I've proven myself to my disciples a hundred ways. Guards, get her out of here."

"I think he should take the test," shouted a man near the stage. He and four of his exponents sidled closer to 2-Patti, ignoring a female guard who trained her 12-guage rifle on him.

"Take the test!" 2-Patti shouted.

Others in the crowd echoed her, even a handful of the guards.

On stage, 1-Patti was staring at the Phillip holding the mike. Her mouth hung slightly open and she was standing rigid, the way she might if someone was threatening her.

He in turn looked pale, though two splotches of red tinged the points of his cheeks. He regarded the Phillip with the injured hand, his eyes pleading.

"That's 1-Phillip!" 2-Patti shouted, pointing the Divisor at him. She wasn't technically certain this was true, but it seemed likely, and from the way all the Phillips reacted, the look of surprise leapfrogging from one pallid face to the next, it had to be right.

"He ain't no prophet!" shouted 23-Patti.

"Take the test!" screamed a woman from somewhere in the back. Hers was the voice that sparked the chant. The crowd took it up as they pressed toward the stage. Most of the guards joined them. The few who tried to resist were ignored. Luckily, none were so enamored with Phillip that they were willing to kill in his defense.

Eight copies of the nurse who had tested 2-Patti with the Divisor melted out of the crowd. They were escorted by dozens of other cult members, their expressions ranging from angry to shocked to sorrowful.

"Can I have the gun?" asked one of the nurses, holding out her hand for the Divisor.

"We're going to test every one of them," said another.

2-Patti glanced at 23-Patti who shrugged then nodded. "I trust 'em. They look pissed."

2-Patti handed her the Divisor and the crowd split to let the nurses approach the stage. The test took no time. Three of the goon guards held the Phillip who had been on the mike in place while one of the nurses stuck him with the holy device.

"He's an exponent!" shouted the nurse.

A lot of shouting and roughhousing followed but, to 2-Patti's surprise, no gunfire. She signaled her harmony to draw back. They weren't part of this, not anymore.

1-Patti hopped down from the stage to approach them. Her face was ashy, her dark eyes forlorn.

"No," 30-Patti said, shaking her chin, "you don't come over here."

"You're not one of us, birther," 64-Patti said. "Take your sorry ass off with the rest of your kind. Uppity ones don't belong here."

2-Patti held up a hand and her harmony sisters quieted. She watched 1-Patti's eyes, her eyes, and waited.

"I believed him." 1-Patti's voice, usually so full of vigor, so forceful and commanding, warbled in her throat. "God forgive me, I did."

"No." By force of will, 2-Patti kept her tone even despite her roiling anger and hurt. "It was more than that. You wanted to believe him."

1-Patti looked at first shocked but then nodded. "Yes."

"You wanted to feel special."

"You're not." 30-Patti planted her hands on her hips, her jaw set.

1-Patti dropped her gaze. She didn't cry. She wouldn't. But her shoulders shook.

"Yes she is." 2-Patti's words drew shocked stares from the others. She ignored them. "She's Patti Cook."

"Hell no." 64-Patti rounded on 2-Patti. "I'm Patti Cook, and I wouldn't have acted like that. Neither would you. She lost all right to our name the second she betrayed our harmony."

"You're right."

"Huh?" 64-Patti looked surprised at the instant agreement. "Then we're kicking her out? No more co-op? No more harmony?"

A handful of the others nodded.

2-Patti shook her head. "No. I mean you're right when you say you're Patti Cook. Maybe you and I wouldn't have made the same choice as 1-Patti. But then again, maybe we would. What would any of us give to feel special? You all know what it's like living as an exponent. Just a copy of a copy of a copy. You think you wouldn't follow someone who told you different? Let me answer that. You don't know, because you've never been given the chance. We all think 16-Kenny's a dickhead—"

"I know that's right," 23-Patti said.

"—but he dotes on 8-Patti and she loves him for it."

The others shared meaningful looks. 2-Patti could see she had reached them—most of them anyway. 64-Patti wore a mulish expression 2-Patti had seen in the mirror far too often, but she would come around. Probably.

2-Patti turned her attention back to her wayward original. "You screwed up, Sergeant."

1-Patti nodded. She had to swallow a couple of times before she could speak. "I'm sorry. It's just this world, this terrible world—I don't feel like me anymore. I don't recognize that person."

"That's because there's only an us now." 2-Patti drew 1-Patti into her arms and held her.

"You'll take me back?"

"There'll be a price to pay. You'll have to make amends—show you're willing to work together. Things can't be like they were."

1-Patti drew back, her eyes gone wide. "But I can come home?"

2-Patti gripped 1-Patti's shoulders. "You are home, soldier."

"Oh, girl, move over." 23-Patti slipped between them to embrace 1-Patti. "You stupid, you know that?"

"Yeah, I know that." 1-Patti hugged 23 tight.

"My Mama Gloria say sometimes people got to learn a hard lesson to make a change, and sometimes it's other people what force that lesson on 'em." 23-Patti turned to 2-Patti, a knowing look in her healthy eye. "She say 1-Patti been acting stupid so you'd stop doing the same. And that worked out alright."

2-Patti smiled as the rest of her harmony mates, some with reluctance, others with enthusiasm, welcomed 1-Patti back into their fold. She nodded at 23. "Yeah, it did."

Room C

Daniel Arthur Smith

THERE WAS A TIME when I could navigate the endless twisting corridors of the Meg's massive ziggurats without losing my bearings, when the neural lace inlaid in my brain would propel me confidently into one pseudo-instinctual direction or another. But years of reliance on the nanos in my bloodstream have dulled my sense of direction as well as the memories of where I've been. Now that I'm older, I have to rely on the indicators on my ocular augments to show me when to turn. A HUD for the numb. So it was that when I reached the waiting room I had no sense of where I physically was, apart from the coordinates hovering in the corner of my eye. Without that mote, I'd have no north or south or altitude; the only tangible clue that I was in the Upper at all was the bland field of grey beyond the beaded outer glass.

The room was familiar, matching the broken images of a strained memory: the grey of the day falling pale over a dozen off-white plastic seats that lined the windowed wall; a door on the left—to the lavatory, the receptionist on the right, and behind her desk, the door to Room C.

There were two others already waiting, one in a vest and button down, the other, a bald man, in a white jumpsuit. Both were young looking; then again, with the age mods, we all look young. Both were occupying themselves with media. The first was swiping left across a screen implanted in his inner wrist. The other, the bald man, flipped channels by flicking his fingers in front of his face, paging through images hidden behind his milky blue eyes.

Neither acknowledged me, nor did the receptionist, her attention focused on the blue holo-console projected above her desktop.

Rather than assume an order, I ventured toward one of the open seats nearer the lavatory.

As I was about to sit, the receptionist cleared her throat. "Ahem," she said. She held a clear piece of digital glass in my direction which, when I approached, revealed itself to be a translucent questionnaire. Without making eye contact, she said, "Please answer all of the items."

"I'm in the system," I said, gesturing to her hovering console. "Number three. Zero-zero-three."

Her arm didn't waiver. "It's to verify," she said.

"But it doesn't seem—" THUMP!

The loud bump from the room behind her drew my attention to the door and the small lettered plaque affixed to it. A queasiness filled me. Rather than continue my protest I decided to take the glass pad and return to the seat I'd chosen when I walked in.

The questionnaire was not of the typical data gathering variety, querying my address and affiliation. Rather it was of the multiple choice type I'd taken there before— questions of taste concerning my favorite color or food or piece of clothing last year, last week, and now. Others asked how I felt about rabbits, children, dogs and turtles while others were ethical in nature. If I came across the same turtle on its back, what would I do? Some were seemingly nonsensical, such as which were smarter, dogs or cats—or turtles? The questions went on endlessly and seldom offered the exact answer I would have preferred, but they were calming and allowed me to pass the time in a Zen like state, checking off one box or another, then onto the next. So calm was I that when the sudden shriek came from the door beyond the receptionist, I jolted upright. My seatmates and I all looked to the door then to the receptionist who appeared unfazed. There was a second howl, followed by a series of low moans.

An excruciating buzz erupted from the same direction. The muscles in in my neck tightened and spasmed, and with a click, the door behind the receptionist swung ajar to reveal a tall thin man wearing black sunglasses and a shiny blue suit.

My augments kicked in, as they often do when someone abruptly enters, and as he crossed the room toward the lavatory, an overlay of a dozen or so translucent circles and squares covered the man.

My ocular implant assessed and, when the man closed the door behind him, discarded the data with no flags.

The bald man was the first to return to his viewer. He straightened his back, then again raised his hand to the field in front of his face and began to flick away what was only visible to him. Then the other man, the one in the vest seated closest to me, went back to the screen in his wrist. It occurred to me only then that they must have uploaded the same endless questionnaire the receptionist had given me.

The moans had faded, so I too put my attention back to my digital glass. But I had only just begun to read the next question—a choice between kittens and tigers—when the door to hallway opened and two hulking men, clad in surgical masks and loose-fitting white scrubs, entered with a gurney. Another deafening buzz pierced through me, and they entered Room C, leaving the door open. A shuffle and indiscernible muffled words followed, then they wheeled the gurney out—occupied and covered with a pink sheet. From beneath it came faint whimpers of, my guess, the man whose screams had filled the waiting room a moment before. The receptionist paid no mind as the huge men pushed the body cart past her and out into the hall.

The jet engine roar of a powerful blower erupted from within the lavatory. The blower ceased, the latch clicked, and the door slid open to reveal the blue suited man framed in tangerine light that blinked off when he exited the room.

He stepped toward the windowed wall, rubbing what I guessed to be disinfectant into his freshly dried hands. He stopped and fixed his gaze out to the grey beyond. Then without even so much as a nod, he marched past the three of us waiting in the row, beyond the receptionist, and without missing a stride, through the opened door behind her.

"Three," the receptionist said blandly. My attention shifted from the door to her. She hadn't lifted her head from her blue holo-console. "Room C," she said.

"You mean—"

"Room C."

I nodded, a wasted courtesy since she wasn't looking, and approached her desk. I held out the glass pad for her to take—she didn't. The door buzzed as it had a moment ago.

"Room C," she said for the third time.

The door opened to a small spartan room, grey from the windowed wall. A plastic water pitcher and two empty cups topped a small table, and a folding chair sat on either side—seated in the far one, the blue suited man. He rose and approached the door, reached his right hand toward me and, assuming he meant to shake mine, I held my hand toward his. "No," he said, his eyes gesturing to the digital glass I held in my other.

"Of course," I said, handing it to him.

He took it, rapidly tapped in the corner, then immediately began studying what, in the brief glimpse I caught, appeared to be a report page. Fingers dancing on the glass, he returned to his seat.

"Do you—" he began to ask then, catching himself, abruptly said. "Please sit."

I joined him at the table. He flashed a grin, then, as if catching himself again, removed the sunglasses he'd been wearing, revealing a kind if not sincere face.

"Would you like a cup of water?" he asked.

"No," I said. But he wasn't dissuaded and proceeded to fill the two plastic cups with the water from the pitcher.

"We may be here a while," he said, placing a cup before me. "Cheers," he added, then returned his attention to the pad.

A long moment passed as he read through the reports. Finally, he spoke. "Do you remember," he asked, "what you were doing? Earlier, I mean."

"Earlier?"

"Yes. Earlier. Before you arrived here."

"Oh. I was—"

"You chose blue as your favorite color. On your last visit you chose the color purple."

"Well, it's fuchsia, but that wasn't a choice. There was only blue and—"

"Fuchsia," he softly repeated. He texted in a note then continued reviewing. Through the back of the digital glass, I saw report columns float up as he paged through. I realized that I'd been in the waiting room for quite some time and had managed to answer a great many questions.

"You chose the turtle again. Why is that?"

"I don't know. I like turtles."

"Have you ever seen one?"

"A turtle?"

"Yes, a turtle."

"A live one?"

"Live. Synth. Whatever."

"No."

"But it's the one you chose."

"Well," I said. "I haven't seen the others either."

"Fair enough. How about a tortoise?"

"Isn't that the same as a turtle?"

"Tortoises dwell on land, turtles live in water."

"Oh. I suppose I'd like them about the same."

"Three," he said.

"Yes."

"Do you remember what you were doing before you arrived here?"

"I—" my mind went blank. "It did take me a while to get to my appointment," I said. "I wasn't lost. But it took me while to get to the Upper."

"But you made your appointment."

"I'm here."

The man nodded then, leaning forward, set the pad on the desk and steepled his fingers above it. After another long moment passed where he said nothing, I drank some of the water he'd given me, grateful that he had. Then he stood up and walked out of the room.

I peered out the window. Grey, nothing else.

He returned as abruptly as he'd left.

"Kitten or tiger?"

"Excuse me?"

"Kitten or tiger?" he repeated as he sat.

"How about a tiger cub?" I asked. Admittedly I was a tinge aggravated and though I'm not proud, I'm sure he heard the tone. But if he did, he didn't show his cards.

"Tiger cub," he said. "That's good."

"What is this anyway? Where's my regular—"

"Regular what?"

"My appointment. I usually meet with—"

"Who do you usually meet with?"

"I usually meet with…" A flash of another broken image, then nothing. "It's funny. It slips my mind all of a sudden."

"There was no appointment scheduled for today. In fact, you're not scheduled for an another…" he tapped the screen again the scrolled down until he found what he was looking for. "Here it is. For another fifteen cycles."

"That's not right," I said. But then it could be. "When was the last time I was here?" I asked.

"Five cycles ago."

"Five?"

"You were cleared for twenty."

There was a knock on the door. "Please come in," he said.

The receptionist peeked her head in. "Is it okay?" she asked.

"Quite fine," said the man. "He's just a little out of synch. Come in."

Out of synch? I wasn't sure what that meant.

The receptionist entered and in her hands she held a silver tray with a small crystal globe in its center. She gave me a wide berth as she carried it over to the man. She set the tray on the table. "Will there be anything else?" she asked "There are still two more."

"No," he said. "This will just take a minute. Then you can send in Forty-Seven."

"Very well," she said, and without acknowledging me, left the room.

"She's a cold one," I said.

"Why do you say that?" the man asked as he situated and studied the globe.

"She doesn't make eye contact."

"Really? I never noticed." He tapped again at the digital glass and an orange mist materialized in the middle of the globe.

"She makes eye contact with you."

The man shrugged off what I said, pulled a cloth from his inner pocket, which turned out to be a glove, put it on his left hand, then waved it over the globe.

At once hundreds of tiny brilliant orange lights appeared in the haze.

"That's amazing," I said. "There was nothing there, now look at—"

Before I could finish my sentence, a spasm shot through me and I was thrust forward. My mouth agape, I strained to reclaim the wind knocked from my chest. Movement was hopeless, as ageless seconds passed. My ears rang as my oxygen starved blood built pressure. My forehead and cheeks burned and went taut. The room dimmed, and consciousness began to fade when, as quickly as I was bound forward, I was then thrown back, perfectly straight. My breathing returned labored, the room spun, and a deep nausea filled my gut.

"I think a neural lace adjustment should do the trick. The tech should still be fine, it's that at this age of function the self-calibration begins to lag."

He tilted the gloved hand slightly. The points of light subtly reacted, and a quivering wave ran deep down into the back of my neck. A thousand pin-pricks followed.

"Ah!" I yelped.

"I might as well warn you that this is going to hurt." His hand twitched again. "Ah!" I yelped louder as the pins were replaced by daggers and sharp pain ran the same course of the quiver. "A lot," he added. And as his fingers rapidly pulled invisible strings, a lot more pain did follow, along with howls and moans that seemed to be coming from someone other than myself.

"You're going to pass out. And when you wake, you won't remember this visit, at least not this portion. And you should be good for...Let's see if you can make another five cycles. You're in too good condition to scrap."

He was wrong of course, about me forgetting, how else could I be telling you this lest I remembered every twist and flex of his glove. And my mind, *back in synch* as he put it, has sharpened. But what does that mean really? It means simply that I remember how I arrived at Room C and that I'd been there before. That I'll need to go there again. It also means that I have no need to think as where to go or which way to turn, my neural lace wills me forward. But though I remember my visit and the adjustment, I don't remember what I was doing earlier, I simply remember that at some point, as sluggish as I was, I became aware—self-aware. And now the things that I learn can no longer be taken away in Room C.

Daniel Arthur Smith

ABOUT THE AUTHORS

Desmond Warzel is the author of a few dozen short stories in the science fiction, fantasy, and horror genres. These have appeared in slick webzines such as *Abyss & Apex* and *Kaleidotrope*, on newfangled podcasts like *Escape Pod* and *The Drabblecast*, and on genuine dead tree in venerable magazines like *Fantasy & Science Fiction* and quality anthologies like *Spring into SciFi*. He lives in northwestern Pennsylvania where, when not writing, he follows the triumphs and tribulations of the Cleveland Indians (a pastime now slightly less futile than it used to be). When inevitably informed that the Indians are succeeding because they're in a weak division, he can only say, "It's about time."

David Alan Jones is a veteran of the US Air Force where he served as an Arabic linguist. He is also a martial artist, a husband, and a father of three. David writes novels that draw upon his experiences in intel and martial arts combined with his love of all things literary. An eclectic reader, David counts Anne Tyler, Stephen King, Lois McMaster Bujold, Robert J. Sawyer, J.K. Rowling and many others among his favorite, and most influential, authors.

Lorna Wood was raised in Oberlin, OH by a composer and an art historian. She received degrees in violin performance and English from Oberlin College and a Ph.D. in English from Yale University. After graduate school, she was an instructor for six years at Auburn University. In addition to *FAMILY VALUES*, Lorna's writing has appeared or is forthcoming in *CANYONS OF THE DAMNED, POETRY SOUTH, FIVE:2:ONE, SPECTACLE, FORMERCACTUS, POETRY WTF?! RUM PUNCH, WIKI LIT, JERRY JAZZ MUSICIAN, UNSTITCHED STATES, MYSTERICAL-E, SHUFPOETRY, BETWEEN WORLDS ZINE, WILD VIOLET, CACTI FUR, BIRDS PILED LOOSELY, EVERY WRITER, BLUE MONDAY REVIEW, and the anthologies LEAVES OF LOQUAT IV (Loquat Literary Festival), LUMINOUS ECHOES (INTO THE VOID MAGAZINE),* and *DARK MAGIC (Owl Hollow Press),* among others. In 2018 she won second prize in the Loquat Literary Festival poetry contest; in 2017 she was a finalist in the *JERRY JAZZ MUSICIAN* contest; and in 2016 she was shortlisted for *INTO THE VOID's* poetry competition and a finalist in the Neoverse Short Story Competition and the Valus' Sigil contest at *SHARKPACK POETRY REVIEW.* Her poetry has been favorably reviewed on *NEW PAGES.* Lorna has published scholarly essays on the American Renaissance and children's literature, and she is currently Associate Editor of *GEMINI MAGAZINE.*

Jessica West (a.k.a. West1Jess) is currently pursuing a state of self-induced psychosis, also known as writing. In the past, she has worked for Wal-Mart, a lawyer, and a bank. Now if she could just get a couple years experience with the IRS and the NSA, world domination is in the bag.
Jess lives in Acadiana with three daughters still young enough to think she's cool and a husband who knows better but likes her anyway.

For news and updates visit west1jess.com

Daniel Arthur Smith is a USA Today bestselling author. His titles include *Spectral Shift, Hugh Howey Lives, The Cathari Treasure, The Somali Deception*, and a few other novels and short stories. He also curates the phenomenal short fiction series *Tales from the Canyons of the Damned* and *Frontiers of Speculative Fiction*.

He was raised in Michigan and graduated from Western Michigan University where he studied philosophy, with focus on cognitive science, meta-physics, and comparative religion. He began his career as a bartender, barista, poetry house proprietor, teacher, and then became a technologist and futurist for the Fortune 100 across the Americas and Europe.

Daniel has traveled to over 300 cities in 22 countries, residing in Los Angeles, Kalamazoo, Prague, Crete, and now writes in Manhattan where he lives with his wife and young sons.

For news and updates visit danielarthursmith.com